Good Cat!

by Cristina Reyes
illustrated by Katherine Potter

Where is that cat?
My cat is on the mat.

Here, cat!
Come here, cat.
Come to play.

Where is that cat?
My cat is in the grass.

Here, cat!
Come here, cat.
Come for a drink.

Where is that cat?
Where can she be?

My cat is on my lap.
Good cat!
Good cat!

Comprehension Check

Retell the Story

Use a Setting and Character Chart to help you retell the story.

Setting	What the Characters Do There

Think and Compare

1. In which room is the cat on the mat? What is the cat doing?

2. Do you like cats? Why or why not?

3. What do cats do that people do?